Galleon Treasures

A collection of poems

SINDHU G RAJESH

First Published in May 2020

ISBN: 978-93-90119-38-7

BLUEROSE PUBLISHERS

www.bluerosepublishers.com

info@bluerosepublishers.com

+91 8882 898 898

Cover Design:

Tyngshain Pariat

Typographic Design:

Ayushi Garg

Distributed by: BlueRose, Amazon, Flipkart, Shopclues

DEDICATION

I dedicate this book to all the young dreamers and achievers and to this beautiful Cosmos.

PREFACE

Memories of this lifetime are so valuable to all. We learn and grow from experiences. As a teenager I used to pen down a lot of my emotions, I used to talk to plants and love to be with nature all the time. This book has evolved with time and touches upon various emotions.

I used to be a great dreamer and wished dreams would just continue as stories and for sometime never realized how connected I would get to it.

When I visited the Jallianwala Bagh, I just wondered what emotions would go through every Indian there if he lived today. I was so proud of the colourful bazaars of India and till today I visit bazaars during festivals just to be present with the colours the flowers and happy emotions.

As I experienced life I went through different emotional patterns and till today I am evolving. Some of my emotions on Girl power and Opportunity lost were all written as I experienced my girlhood days.

Being a mother now I often wonder if my child would be able to connect to nature as much as I did. I never did feel that need to complain or discuss what I felt at every point of my life. I called them all special moments and converted them to sweet poems. Today I am willing to share with all my readers a bit of that everything I felt in those EVERYDAYS.

ACKNOWLEDGEMENT

I thank each and everyone who has inspired me to make this book a possibility. I thank my husband, my daughter and my parents who have immensely supported me with what ever I do. I specially thank my friend Zohara Sultan and Saloni Bhatia who have given me a loads of encouragement and made me feel special about this new journey.

I thank all my facilitators of Access Consciousness.

Thanks to Blue Rose publications for publishing this book for me.

I thank God and this Universe for giving me special moments in my life,ones which I faced with tears and joy and which have helped me grow as a person.

CONTENTS

Unravelling the treasures......truly from the heart.

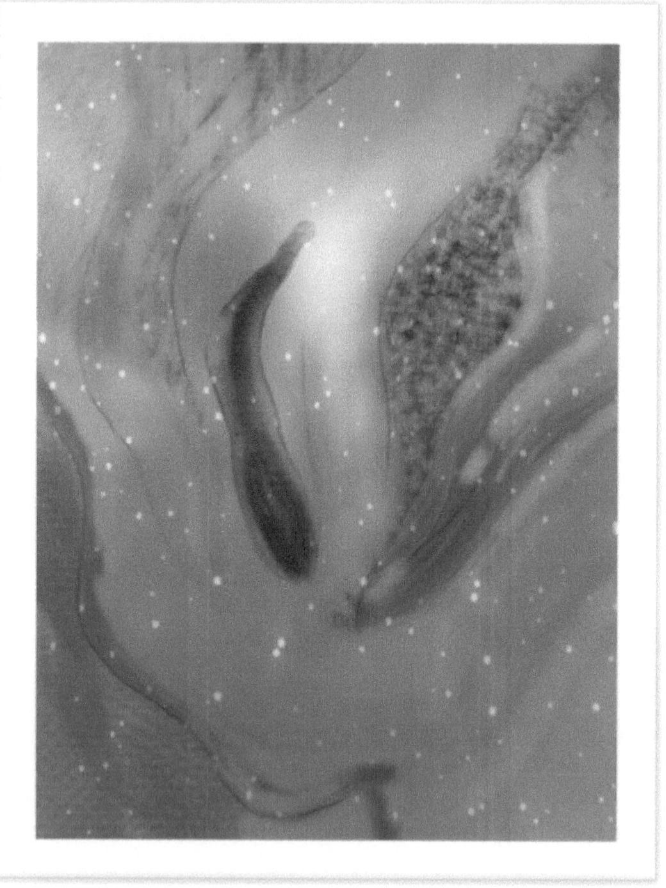

DREAMS

Dreams are never a reality
Dreams reflect our minds
Dreams are always unkind

You can be a queen in a dream
You can be a pauper say..
You can look beautiful and
Look very ugly too.
But dreams are never a reality.

A dream can make you sad
It can make you joyous through
A dream can depress you
It can excite you too
But Dreams only reflect your mind.

You can be a rich man
A poor man you can be
You get your wishes answered
Get yourself haunted grey

But dreams are dreams
They are always unkind.

They leave you with an impression
But can never look behind
It looks touched and lived
But never with you in time.
Dreams reflect our mind.

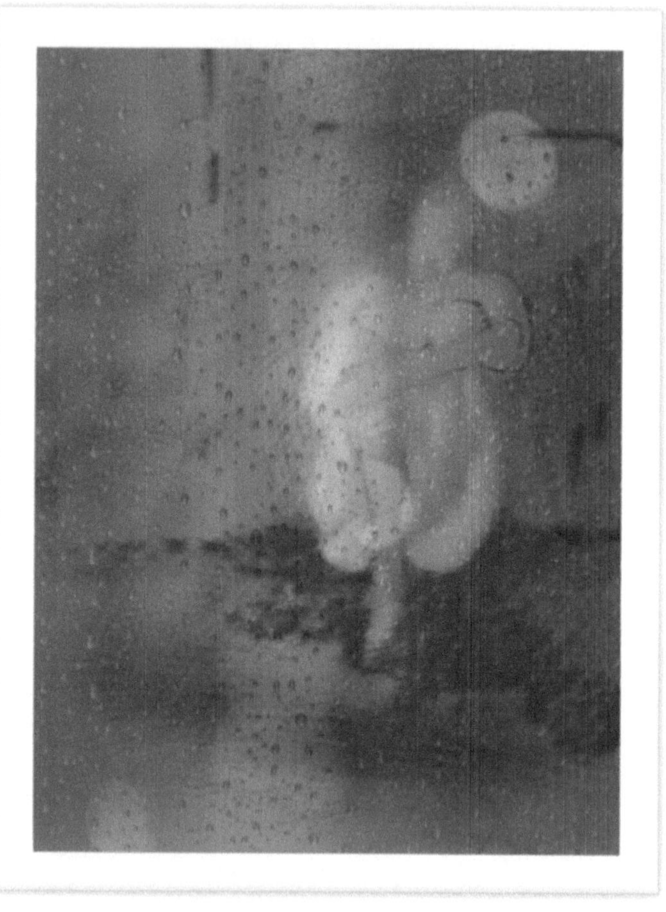

LONELINESS

It was a night of peace and harmony
Owls hooting, the bustle of the trees
catches the ear;
The silver moon spreads its light among the trees
Gleamed by its light upon a fair cheek was a sorrowful tear
The night was so quiet so helpful to her cause she needed peace.
No one could hear her no-one could see her
Why should she bother, she was accompanied by her dear.
Her lovely friend he was her only beloved
No one could cheat her of him
He too wouldn't leave her, he belonged to her, only beloved
She hated him, but nurtured him
Loved him and never ignored him.
She knew he was her only beloved
He never argued,only listened
He never spoke only made her think
His silence was something she loved.
"Till my grave will you come?" she pleaded,
To which he only heeded.
Years passed by and in the bed of roses she lay
Tears of every soul fell there.
She was wrinkled tanned and worn
But their friendship could never be torn.
In her grave she lay smiling,
He lay with her, beside her.
Great is their love and praise to this love.
From childhood to grave, he accompanied her.
He was hers, her Loneliness alone.
She loved you Loneliness.

CHILDHOOD

Childhood dear!

You are simple pure and honest,
You are the best and the quickest
You come once in a lifetime.

You made me sing a nursery rhyme
Time will not go back nor do the years
Challenges come to increase my fears.
I do miss you, just want to touch you
You are within me, though I may turn new
You are the first phase of my life
You have the most valuable price.

You made me ride
A merry go round, a carousel,a swing
Happiness was the only thing.
Seldom I cried,little did I whine
Was always sure you are divine.
You are the first phase of my life
You have the most valuable price.

Oh Childhood how I yearn for thee!

FREEDOM

Do you hear that cry of Joy
It's a cry of freedom
From every Indian toy
The culture breaks its way free
It flows in different colours
Celebrations you can see
The English blood stops it's flow
And every Indian has a right to know
His name, tradition, friend and foe
The rivers of India dash and flow
The mountains show their peaks with pride
And every sea celebrates its high tide
Every bird sings along its way
Every forest celebrates this day
Thanks to the leaders Gandhi and all
At last Freedom has answered their call.

MY COLOURFUL INDIA

Lucky to be in this land called treasure,
Cultures,races and colours are its pleasure.
Festivals of joy take pride in its play
When every Indian is happy and gay!
Dolaks and drums catches every ear,
Music and dance washes off every tear.
Ghagras and sarees in silk and gold gleam;
To look ethnic is every Indians dream.
Every direction has a contrast:
Fixed are its features from the very past.
The bazaars of India have its own features
Streets, lanes and gullies form a colourful picture
Colourful cities, fortresses and gates
Echoes in all ears the kingly fates.
Learn India and then just see,
Why an Indian I'm proud to be.

LITTLE VIOLET

It was a fine morn,when I took a small stroll,
I found a small violet near a tall pole.
I looked and felt,just a violet it could be
Why should it be any cause to me?
Every morning I would find it there,
Bloomed and beautiful in the mud bare
But I just looked and felt,just a violet it could be
Why should it be any cause to me.
My morns and evenings just went by
There was not a day without some joy!
Soon enough I found a secret,
Ran to the violet ,just to pick it
And LO!
Just a violet it would be.
Single violets are luck I found
When I reached there it was just a bare mound.
The entire vine was uprooted
No more violets I could find
Even now I take a stroll,
Hoping to see a violet near the pole
Luck can you ever shine on me?
The secret violet I would love to foresee.
Never would I think just a violet it could be,
Because it made a strong cause to me.
Friends, Violets you should never ignore
Joy in your life it's sure to pour.

LAMP CALLED LOVE

If there is Darkness in your Life be sure
There is a lamp to light it up
Search till you find this happiness
Merge in this light and it's warmth
One day you will know the worth of it
Both in big ways and in small
The lamp of love I have found
It's glow beginning to rise
I protect it from the wind and rain
And ease away all my hidden pain
I would walk my path with pleasure
Knowing this light is my treasure
This light and I found with great delight
Unaware of its bounds.
I protect it from the wind and rain
And sink in its warmth and glow
This love will be forever and forever more.

WITHIN ME

When miles are crossed and hopes are lost,
A wave rises in your mind
You shiver and tremble,and in deepest thoughts
You realise I'm calm within.
You close your eyes , then open them again
You see,a light shines far across:
You begin again with a smile.
You crawl, then gently walk
Slowly all your fears seems crossed.
Cramped up in your thoughts
You could never see this light within.
Let your eyes of life open again
To see that divine light.
For once you know that beautiful light
Then all your paths will be turned right.

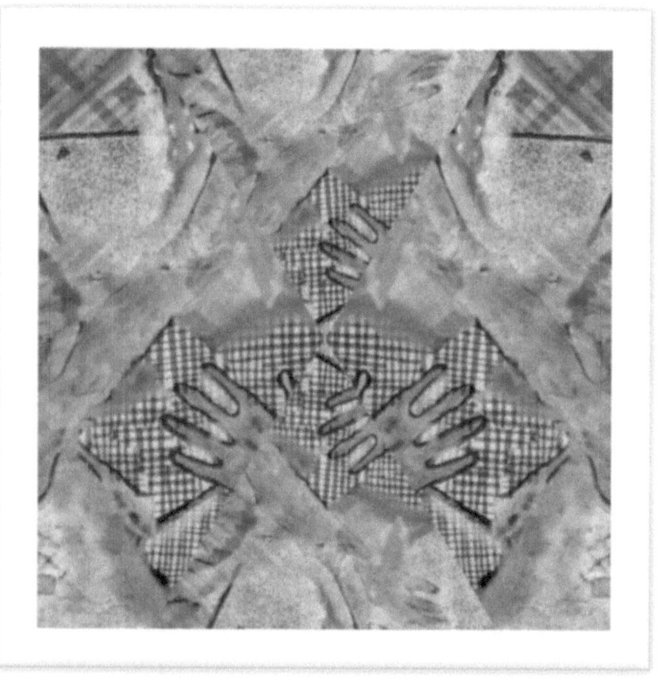

WOUNDED SOLDIER

It once again taps my hearts door
For an answer to its call.

The call was made but the answer gave
No sounds, no sights, no signs.

The door within was locked.
Oh would it open ever again?

All keys to it seemed lost...

Some vague emotions answer
It never seemed to touch the heart.

The key might be found soon someday
To unlock it back again.

Where can I look to find
My dreams and willful pleasure?

Oh !come my savior come back with the key
Break this silence and treat my wound,

This wound in my heart,my mind and destiny.
I would find the key to it and
Cherish it till it's flourished

Would have it till dooms day
With all its youth and pleasure

To Serve my country another time.
For or my heart will never be mine.

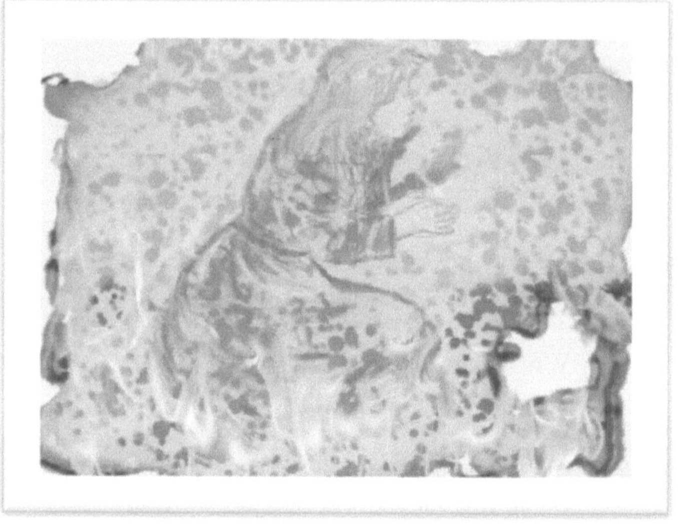

A BROKEN HEART

A gentle wind blew there
Carrying a little fog.
The road was clear
Birds chirped so near
Whispers only one could hear
Trees seemed still as rock.
Ages they have seen
The gate never seemed so far away....
Thorny shrubs grew all around
Silent screeches were the only sound.
The gate creaked when opened
Little had the building changed
The grey walls seemed as solid stone
Never would it smile.
An old broken door had seen
Men walk in and out a heredity
The panes were broken half and hung.
Desks and benches scattered,
Dust strewn all around.
Darker and thicker turned the ground
Candles scattered all around the altar
Glasses wine less bare
The wounded lord looked hurt again,

But on the altar lay
Wishes of a man who lived
Lived and died his happy days
Never which was told ,for he was ghost today.
The man was slain on his wedding
Drops of blood must remain here...
His head was slain down to a corner
His trunk lay torn and bare
The bride was lifted off the floor
And taken far away.
She was hit , she screamed of pain
Churned by thousand beasts
Her life was all in vain.
She would come back ,then she promised
From all the pain to name.
She grew up as a tigress
And hunted all her preys.
It took her years to conquer
Her one and only game
She walked towards the altar
Knelt on the dirty floor,
Give me an answer she prayed
Had she sinned so badly to face life all so sore
A stick she lit and then
Threw it on the floor

Before there was an answer
She was there no more
With the building was burning
Not a body full of life,but
Her dreams, her hopes and smiles
The world would blame her
But she would be a broken heart forever.

AFTER THAT DAY

Just like a flower that sheds away
Just like a colour that fades away
You darkened my life and found your own way
I'm living hard without you
Enlighten and take my soul away
Seasons are dull without you
They change I guess, but I never know
You were the wonderful dream of my life
Brightness and glamour you would always arise
But never again can I find you
Lost in this cave of wither less bound
Stranded in this desert I no longer see
My life here for no reason to be
I no longer feel wise,no senses in reality
When something is lost,life is so tough
You made it that way for me
Give me another spring,another summer or winter
For I'm longing to be free,with a life only for me.

THE COSMOS

The undying heaven and the undying dew
The uneven hills and valleys too
Have their own miseries and sorrows through
This is the solace
A place for human soul
Wonderful in its splendour
Wonderful as a whole
Life's creations are many
Both big and small
Good things always answer, every humans call.
This world of all pleasures
With many hidden treasures
Only pretty things.
One can find contentment forever
Sorrow it never brings
Portions maybe spent in tears
Some maybe in pain
Bundles of joy always remain
Make them all your gain
Truth of life you can always face
Miseries you can keep in pace
Get the essence of this game
And sorrows will never remain
The undying heaven and the undying dew
The uneven hills and valleys too
Have their own sorrows and miseries too.

GIRL POWER

A pretty little flower you are
An everblooming scented one.
You cease a heart so easily
With a power towards ecstasy.
Like no other girl you just smile
A smile with so much purity.
Innocent I would tell you are
When you roll your eyes so big.
Under those lashes beautifully thick
A thunder struck my mind;
When I think what I may later find
You' ll never be forever young,
Tests in life may always come.
One day your innocence will surely die
And you"ll be just another one.
Count on me to tell you this
No soul has ever lasting bliss.
But all these paths have ups and downs
You can trod them one by one.
Take each step with confidence
And let everyone believe
You are not a mere flower,
A timid and a delicate one.
Bring out all your brightness
Give all a helping hand.
Keep your innocence forever matched
With a sparkling smile.
He will do the rest for you
Then your future goes hand in hand.

OPPORTUNITY LOST

As the cold wind blew
I hugged my coat and walked the lane,
To find a bus to take me home.
And as I crossed the street I found
Her sitting all alone.
Nate was so naughty bright
Her face was crystal clear.
She was squatting in the street
Her arms so bare and cold.
Her bowl was empty and so was she
With all unestablished goals
She may have wanted to be a politician!
But little did she know
Her aims are so flimsy,
And stories always untold.
She hugged her rug so close to her
As the cold wind blew
Her hair was tangled in its flow
Devoid of a comb
She may have wanted to be a princess!
But little did she know
Her aims would only defuse her
To a hawker and nothing more.
She laughed at all the passerby's
And glared at them sometimes,
She never recollected her yesterdays,

Her past was never known.
Would someone tell her from where she hailed?
And give her back her home.?
She may have wanted to be a someone
Only does she know,
What made her now so empty and so unknown
Nate picked her bowl and walked passed me
Carrying all the rags she found.
I named her Nate and then looked to see
My bus was going ahead of me...

ABOUT THE AUTHOR

Sindhu G Rajesh is an entrepreneur from Bangalore. Born in the scenic hills of Nilgiris she is a nature lover.Creation is constant and this book is an attempt to explore her creative side of writing.She loves painting landscapes and it a great promoter of arts.

Her company Shrishti Landscapes is one of the leading landscape firms doing lot of work across South India.

Her love for creative writing began with small attempts at school and today as she helps her daughter she still feels alive the little child within her.This book is an attempt to make one realise that all situations that we go through in life are valuable and we can convert all those little moments to treasures.

I had for long hid these poems away and thus I call it Gulleon treasures hidden away somewhere but today I'm making an attempt to share it with the world.

www.ingramcontent.com/pod-product-compliance
Ingram Content Group UK Ltd.
Pitfield, Milton Keynes, MK11 3LW, UK
UKHW040014200726
13854UKWH00001B/189

9 789390 119387